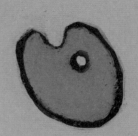
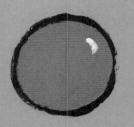

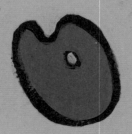
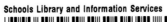

CLEO'S COLOUR BOOK

Caroline Mockford

Barefoot Books
Celebrating Art and Story

Cleo is looking at colours today.

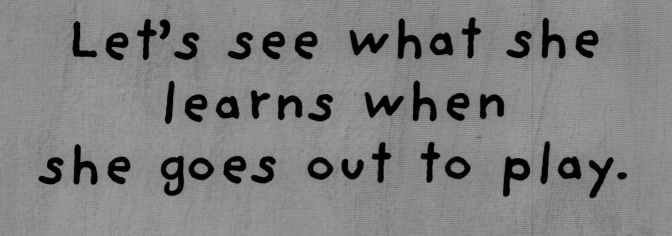

Let's see what she learns when she goes out to play.

Here is a bicycle,
shiny and red.

Here is a flower with
a round yellow head.

Here are some plums,

all
purple
and sweet.

And here's some pink ice cream, delicious to eat!

Here's a small dog
with a big orange ball.

And here's a black kitten on my garden wall.

Here are some apples, all crunchy and green.

And here is a bath
and a
blue submarine.

Here is a bear,
all cuddly and brown.

And here's the white moon shining over the town.

There are so many colours

that Cleo can see.

Try mixing your own
and share
them with me!

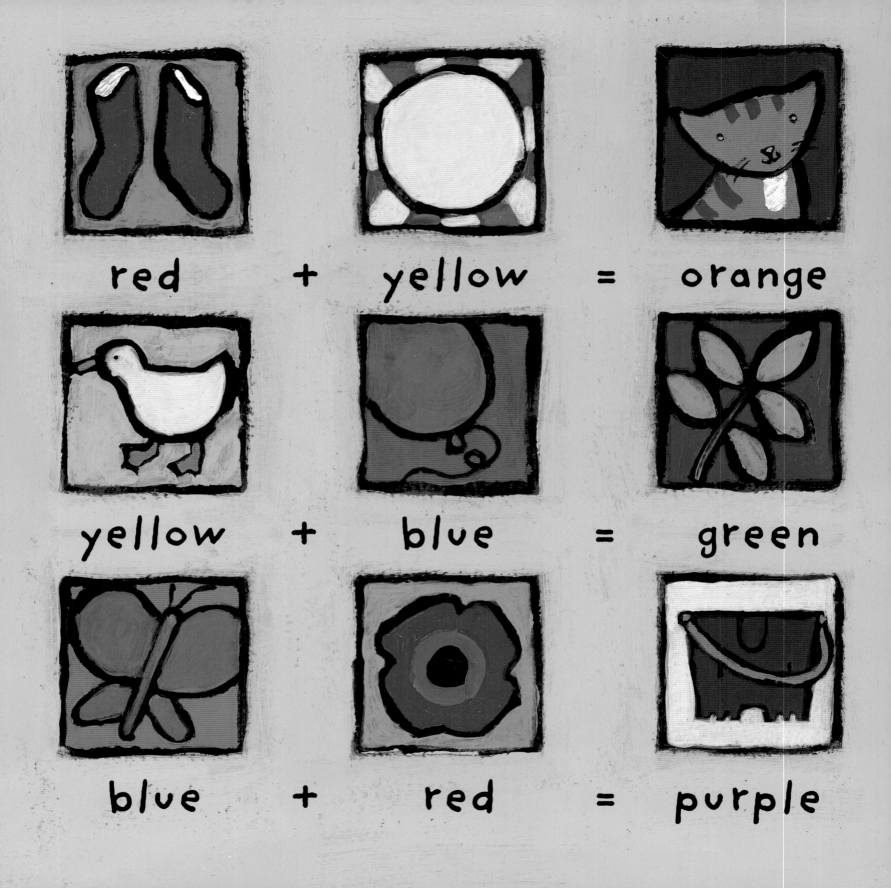

red + yellow = orange

yellow + blue = green

blue + red = purple

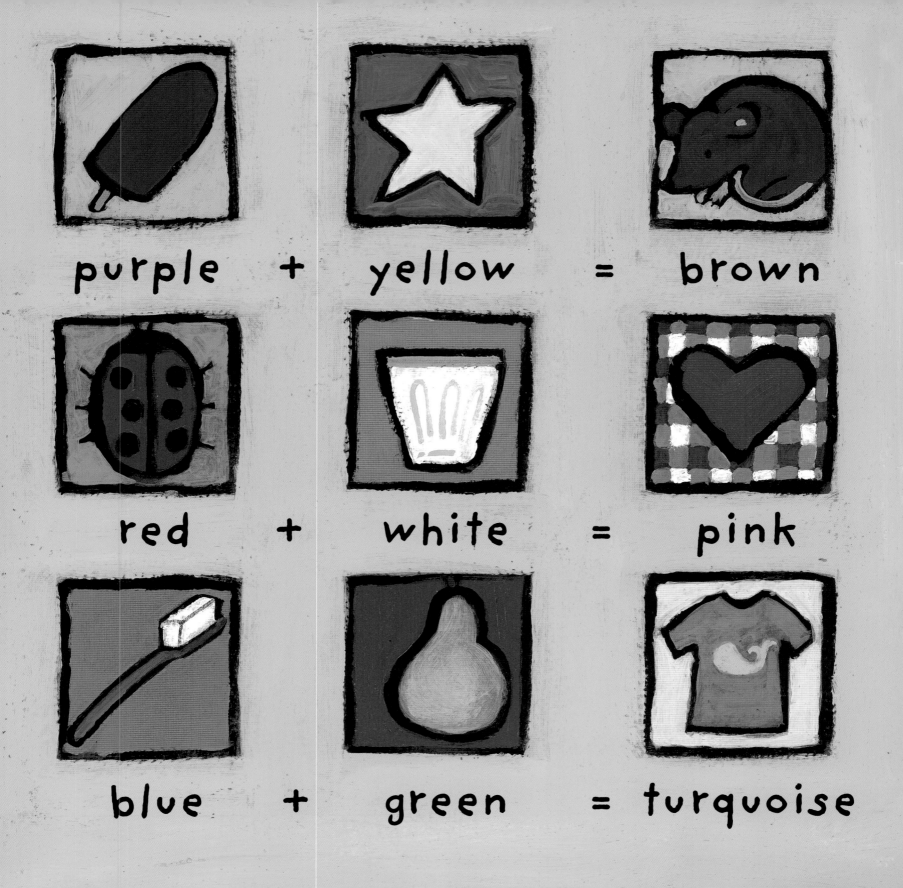

purple + yellow = brown

red + white = pink

blue + green = turquoise

For Jemima — S. B.
For Reuben — C. M.

Barefoot Books
124 Walcot Street
Bath BA1 5BG

This book is printed on 100% acid-free paper
The illustrations were prepared in acrylics on 140lb watercolour paper
Design by Barefoot Books, Bath. Typeset in 44pt Providence Sans Bold
Colour separation by Bright Arts, Singapore
Printed and bound by South China Printing Co. Ltd

Hardback ISBN 1-905236-29-8

British Cataloguing-in-Publication Data:
a catalogue record for this book is available from the British Library

1 3 5 7 9 8 6 4 2

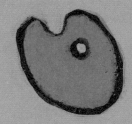

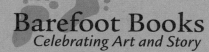
Barefoot Books
Celebrating Art and Story

At Barefoot Books, we celebrate art and story that opens
the hearts and minds of children from all walks of life, inspiring
them to read deeper, search further, and explore their own creative gifts.
Taking our inspiration from many different cultures, we focus on themes that
encourage independence of spirit, enthusiasm for learning, and sharing of
the world's diversity. Interactive, playful and beautiful, our products
combine the best of the present with the best of the past to
educate our children as the caretakers of tomorrow.

www.barefootbooks.com

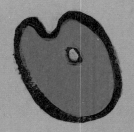